Bella

Thomas

Miranda

Katy

Mrs. Day

Harriet

Lucy

Amy

Ling

Emily

Miss Jane

George

To Rebecca

Text and illustrations copyright © Edwina Riddell 1993

First published in Great Britain in 1993 by
Frances Lincoln Limited, Apollo Works
5 Charlton Kings Road, London NW5 2SB

British Library Cataloguing in Publication Data
available on request

ISBN 0-7112-0789-5 hardback
ISBN 0-7112-0800-X paperback

Set in Helvetica Textbook Roman
Printed and bound in Hong Kong

1   3   5   7   9   8   6   4   2

My first ballet class

Edwina Riddell

Hello! My name is Katy.

FRANCES LINCOLN

Here I am with my best book. It's about ballet. I want to be a dancer when I am big enough.

One day Mum said I was old enough for ballet classes. I gave her a big hug. Then we went to buy the things I needed.

On Saturday, Mum took me to the class. I met Mrs Day, the teacher, and Miss Jane who plays the piano.

There were lots of children there getting changed.

First of all Mrs Day told us to get up and make a circle. She asked us to point our toes like her.

Then we had to point our toes and skip. I felt shy, but I laughed when Thomas bumped into Bella.

Mrs Day showed us how to do good toes and naughty toes.
Good toes point nicely – naughty toes turn up!

We all wiggled our toes and tried not to fall over. Some people's toes are always being naughty.

We learned how to stand in first position. A girl called Miranda knew already, and showed off to us.

I got muddled, but I did it in the end. Bella went all wobbly and knocked Harriet over.

Next we pretended we were ponies and trotted round the room.
We had to point our toes and lift our knees up high.

Mrs Day said, "Trot like dainty ponies, not cart-horses."
Emily thought she was the best pony.

We sat down and listened to Miss Jane playing the piano.
Then we clapped our hands in time to the music.

We had to shout loudly, "ONE, TWO, THREE, FOUR!"
"Not so loud!" said Mrs Day, "I can't hear the piano."

The last thing we learned was how to curtsey. We held our skirts out and copied Mrs Day. The boys bowed instead.

I like ballet class. I want to come again next week.

first position

second position

third position

fourth position

fifth position

first position

second position

third position

fourth position

fifth position